For Olai

PHOTO CREDITS
Pages 8–9: Spencer Sutton/Science Source; Pages 10–11: Brian J. Skerry/National Geographic Creative; Pages 12–13: Copyright © David Wrobel/Seapics.com; Pages 14–15: Chris Newbert/Minden Pictures/National Geographic Creative; Pages 16–17, 33: Joshua Lambus/The Maka Project; Pages 18–19, 32–33: Copyright © Lia Barrett; Pages 20–21, 32: Norbert Wu/Minden Pictures/National Geographic Creative; Pages 22–23: Copyright © David Wrobel/Seapics.com; Pages 24–25: Kerryn Parkinson © NORFANZ Founding Parties; Pages 26–27, 32: Joshua Lambus/The Maka Project; Pages 28–29, 32–33: Courtesy Ines Martin—Deutsches Meeresmuseum; Pages 30–31: Copyright © David Wrobel/Seapics.com

Balzer + Bray is an imprint of HarperCollins Publishers.

The Blobfish Book
Copyright © 2016 by Jessica Olien
All rights reserved. Manufactured in China.
No part of this book may be used or reproduced in any manner whatsoever without written permission except in the case of brief quotations embodied in critical articles and reviews. For information address HarperCollins Children's Books, a division of HarperCollins Publishers, 195 Broadway, New York, NY 10007.
www.harpercollinschildrens.com

Library of Congress Control Number: 2015948268
ISBN 978-0-06-239415-6

Typography by Aurora Parlagreco
16 17 18 19 20 SCP 10 9 8 7 6 5 4 3 2 1
❖
First Edition

Jessica Olien

THE BLObFiSH BOOK

BALZER + BRAY
An Imprint of HarperCollins Publishers

LEARN more about ME!

AUTHOR Jessica Olien

TITLE The Deep Sea Book

DATE DUE	BORROWER'S NAME
JAN 27	
FEB 07	

This way to BLOBFISH

The deepest parts of the ocean are too far for any sunlight to reach.

Zones of the Ocean

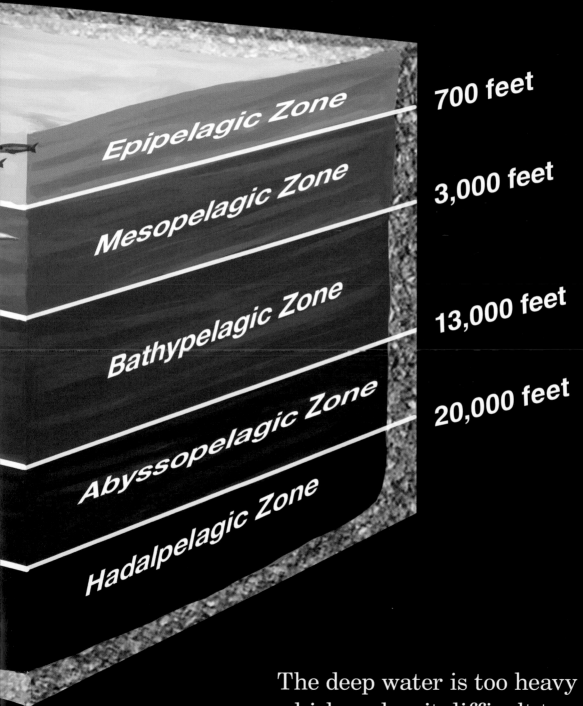

Epipelagic Zone — 700 feet

Mesopelagic Zone — 3,000 feet

Bathypelagic Zone — 13,000 feet

Abyssopelagic Zone — 20,000 feet

Hadalpelagic Zone

The deep water is too heavy for humans, which makes it difficult to explore.

Scientists study sea life miles beneath the surface of the ocean. *Submersibles* are underwater vehicles used to explore the deep sea.

Hi there! Um, do you know if there are going to be any blobfish in this book?

The **viperfish** has such big teeth it can't close its mouth.

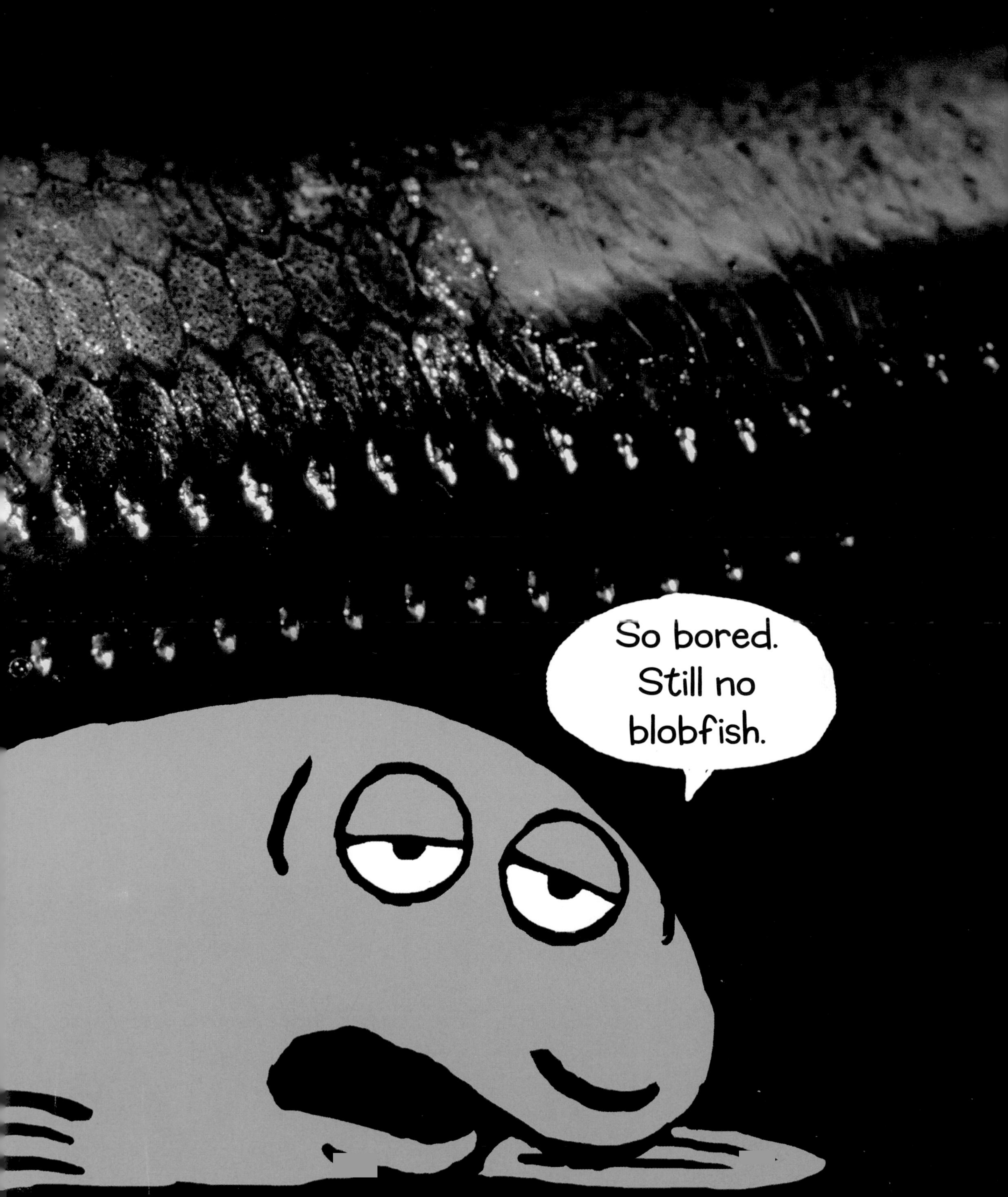
So bored. Still no blobfish.

Some fish have very large eyes to help them see in the dark.

Other fish can't see at all and rely on other senses, such as touch and smell, to guide them.

What about BLOBFISH? Do I have big eyes?

Many deep-sea animals glow in the dark.
This is called *bioluminescence*.

This **jellyfish** lights up to attract food in the dark water.

This **jewel squid** got its name from the photophores all over its body that make it shimmer and sparkle underwater.

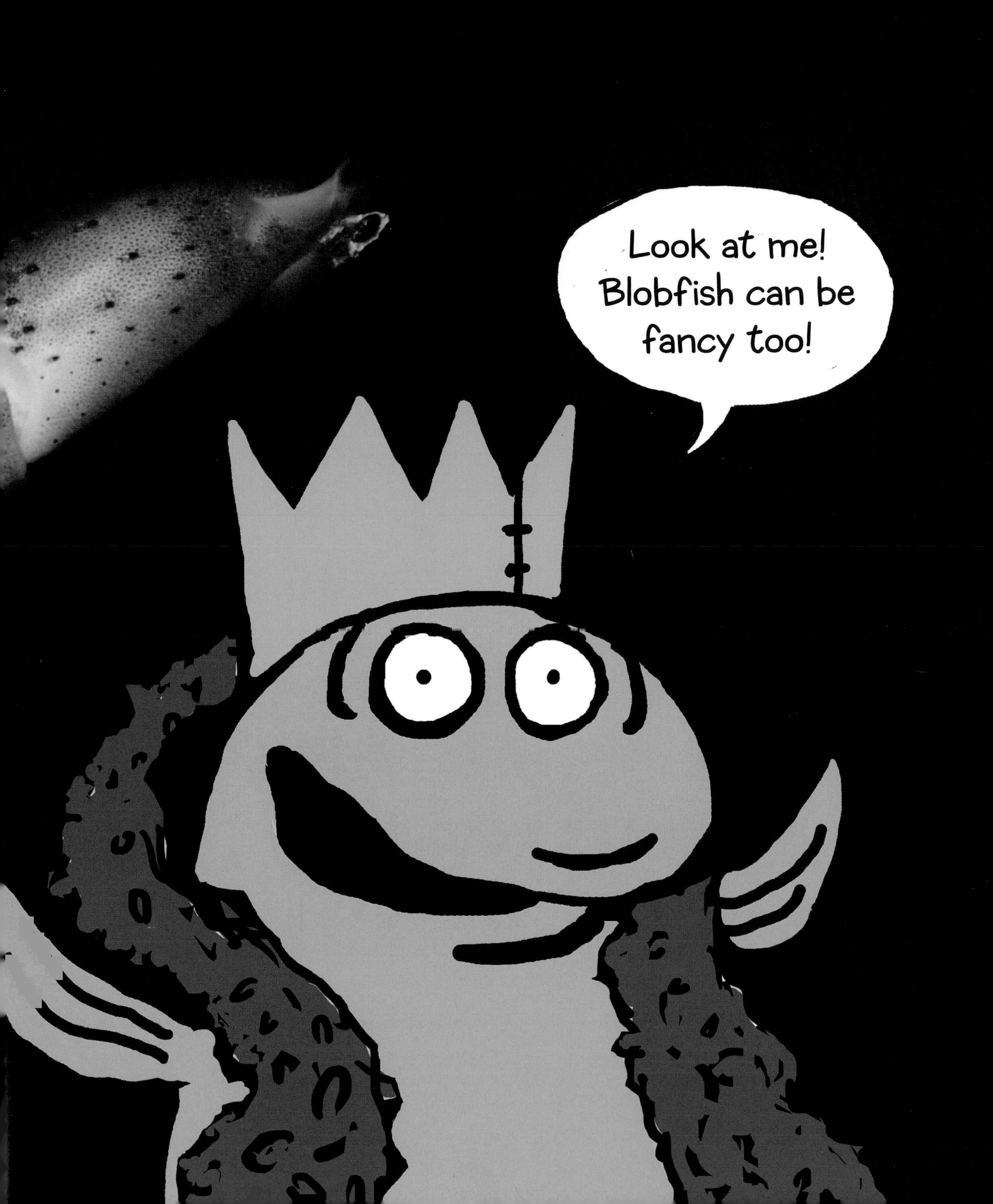
Look at me! Blobfish can be fancy too!

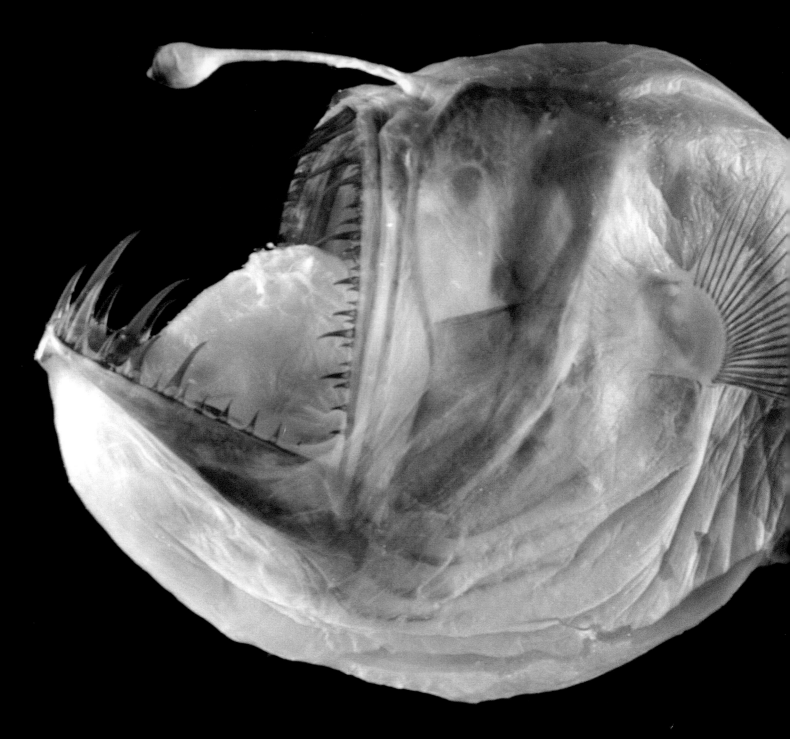

The **anglerfish** has a long fin like a fishing line
on its face with a light on the end to attract other fish.

The **blobfish** has a very soft body that helps it float in the deep water.

The blobfish was once voted the world's ugliest animal.

IT'S ME! Look, everyone! It says BLOBFISH!

Blenny fish come in all different colors, and some people even have them as pets.

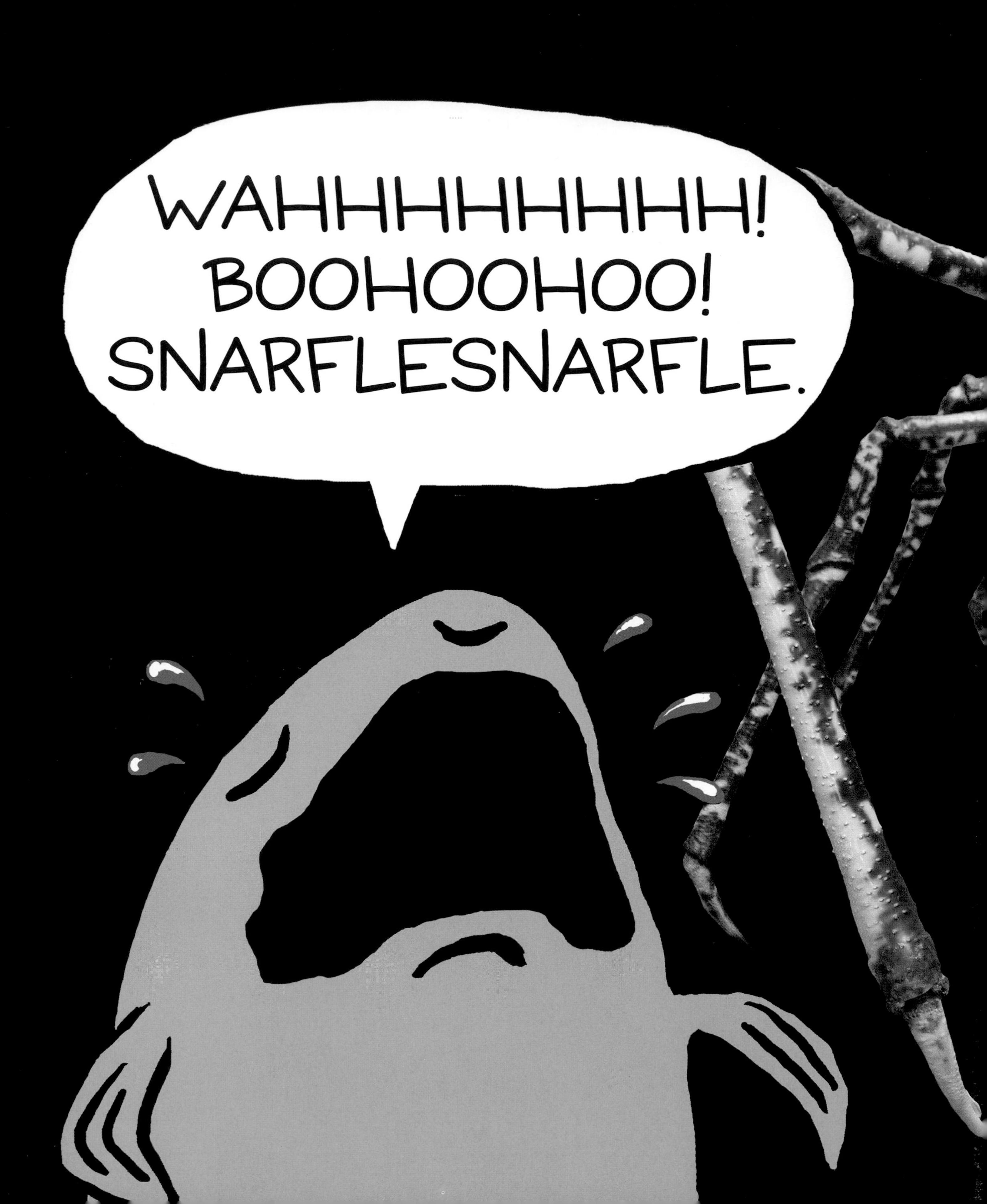
WAHHHHHHHHH! BOOHOOHOO! SNARFLESNARFLE.

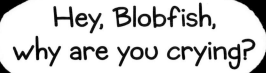

The **giant spider crab** can grow to be twelve feet long from claw to very strong claw.

That is the same size as a small car.

The **northern stoplight loosejaw** can unhinge the bottom of its mouth to take bigger bites.

I know how you feel. Everyone thinks I'm scary, but I'm really small and nice. It's just because people don't understand you.

These animals all coexist deep in the ocean where no plants or sunshine are found.

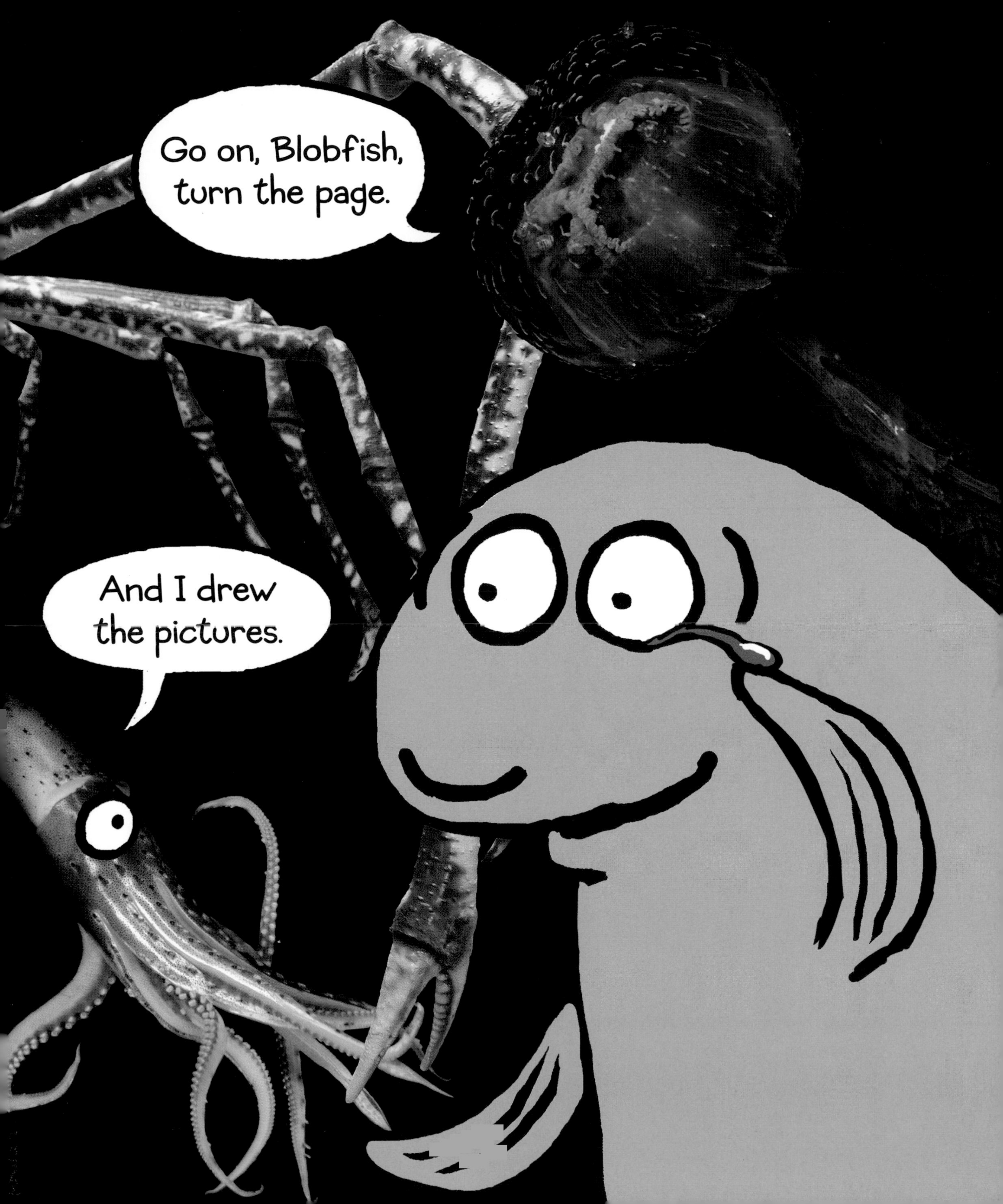
Go on, Blobfish, turn the page.
And I drew the pictures.

CAST OF CHARACTERS

- **Giant spider crabs** can live to be a hundred years old and are known to be very gentle and nice. They decorate their shells with sea sponges and other deep-sea animals.

- **Jellyfish** have been on earth for at least 500 million years.

- The **viperfish** has giant teeth but is really very small—about twelve to twenty-four inches. It has photophores that light up to attract other fish.

- There are two hundred different kinds of **anglerfish**. Only the female anglerfish have a fin like a fishing line on their heads.

- The **jewel squid** has mismatched eyes; one has more sparkles than the other.

- The **northern stoplight loosejaw** looks scary, but it mostly eats just plankton.

- **Blenny fish** live near the ocean floor. They can be in the deep sea or in shallow water.

- If you touched a **blobfish**, it would feel a lot like Jell-O. Being so squishy helps the blobfish float near the bottom of the ocean. Deep-sea fishing, called trawling, hurts the blobfish and its home. Because of this the blobfish is an endangered species.

MORE AMAZING DEEP-SEA FACTS!

• All life on earth started in the ocean.

• More people have walked on the moon than on the bottom of the ocean.

• If you put Mount Everest in the deepest part of the ocean, its tallest point would be more than a mile beneath the surface.

• Because there is no sunlight, it is impossible for plants to live in the deep sea.

• While most life on earth gets energy from the sun, some animals get their energy from thermal vents deep in the water.

Maybe you can help find one of us!

• The ocean pressure is so strong in the deep sea that being down there would feel like you were holding up fifty jumbo jets with your bare hands.

• There are likely many animals in the deep sea that haven't been discovered yet.

READ MORE ABOUT IT
IN THESE SELECTED RESEARCH SOURCES!

Science Daily: Jellyfish
www.sciencedaily.com/releases/2007/10/071030211210.htm

Deep-Sea Creatures: Viperfish
http://deepseacreatures.org/viperfish

National Geographic: Jewel squid
http://news.nationalgeographic.com/news/2007/08/photogalleries
/sea-creatures/photo2.html

National Geographic: Anglerfish
http://animals.nationalgeographic.com/animals/fish/anglerfish/

Encyclopedia Britannica: Blenny fish
www.britannica.com/animal/blenny

Science Direct: Northern stoplight loosejaw
www.sciencedirect.com/science/article/pii/S0967063705001652

National Marine Fisheries Service: Blobfish
www.nmfs.noaa.gov/rss/podcasts/weirdfins/blobfish.htm

The Smithsonian: Blobfish
www.smithsonianmag.com/smart-news/in-defense-of-the-blobfish-why-
the-worlds-ugliest-animal-isnt-as-ugly-as-you-think-it-is-6676336/?no-ist